Harley and the Egg

Written by Malinda Mitchell

Illustrated by Corey Colombin

Tex Ware
Everett, WA

© 2013 Malinda Mitchell and Corey Colombin

All Rights Reserved

No part of this publication may be reproduced, stored in a retrieval system or transmitted in any way by any means—electronic, mechanical, photocopy, recording or otherwise—without the prior permission of the copyright holder, except as provided by USA copyright law.

This book is fiction in its entirety. Any similarities to names of people, places, animals, or books written in the past or present are coincidental.

ISBN-13: 978-1523837656

ISBN-10: 1523837659

Note from the Author:

I wrote Harley and The Egg because I feel that children should be taught from infancy to respect life. What better way to teach children to respect life than with a small egg and another small form of life such as an adorable miniature dachshund as a teacher.

Harley shows love when he sees a small egg and immediately decides to care for it as if it were his own.

Harley loves life without prejudice. It doesn't matter to him what is inside that egg, he just knows that whatever form of life it is that it deserves a chance and he is determined to give it that chance and to love it.

My little red miniature dachshund inspired me to write, *Harley and the Egg*, by being the sweetest little dog any animal lover could ever hope to welcome into their home and family.

My little Harley loves everyone without prejudice. He can say, no, Nana, and he shakes his head no when he doesn't want something and yes when he does.

I also want to thank Corey Colombin for capturing the sweetness of my little Harley through her marvelous illustrations.

A very special thanks to each of you who supported the publication of this book. You have helped make this book a success! It is with great pleasure that I've included your names or the names of your loved ones to this book.

Alexis Weinkauf	Pam Roth O'Mara
Becky Hyatt	Pike Walker Fogle
Emily Schultz	Pinky
In memory of Bella Oakes	Susan Wigden
June Oakes	W. Grant Murray

I also thank Ray Ruppert, the greatest ever publisher, who has worked diligently with Corey and me to make this book the best ever.

Harley was an adorable red miniature dachshund. He enjoyed playing outside, chasing cats, and getting into mischief.

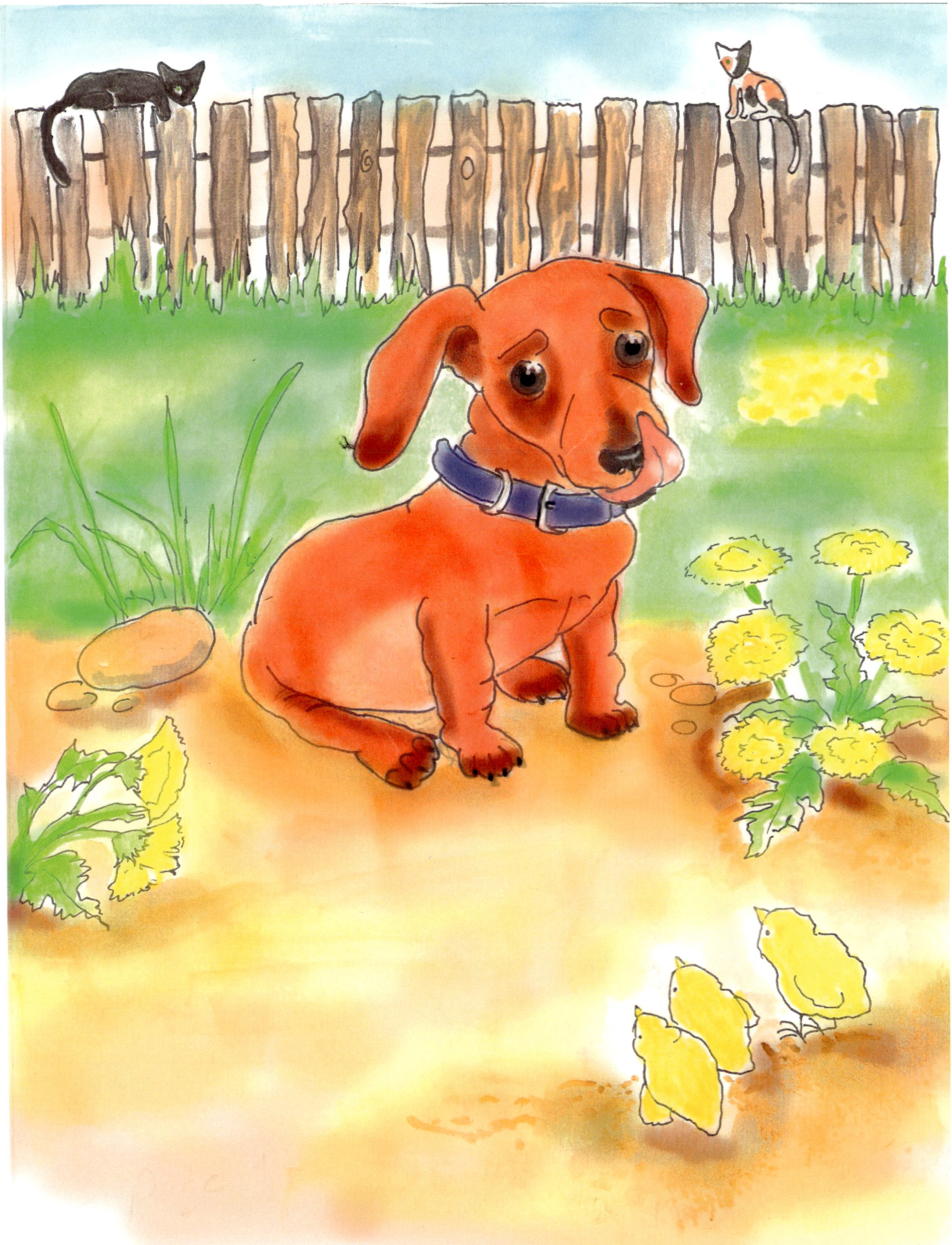

One lovely summer day after much begging, Harley's mother let him go outside alone. Harley promised his mother that he would stay close to home and wouldn't get too close to the cats. She said, "Harley, those cats are bigger than you, and you annoy them with your constant barking and running towards them. One day they will slap you and then maybe you'll understand what I've been trying to tell you. The cats have sharp claws and they could hurt you."

Harley said, "But Mother, I just want to play with the cats. I won't hurt them."

"Harley, please do as I say and stop annoying the cats."

"Okay Mother. I'll leave the cats alone."

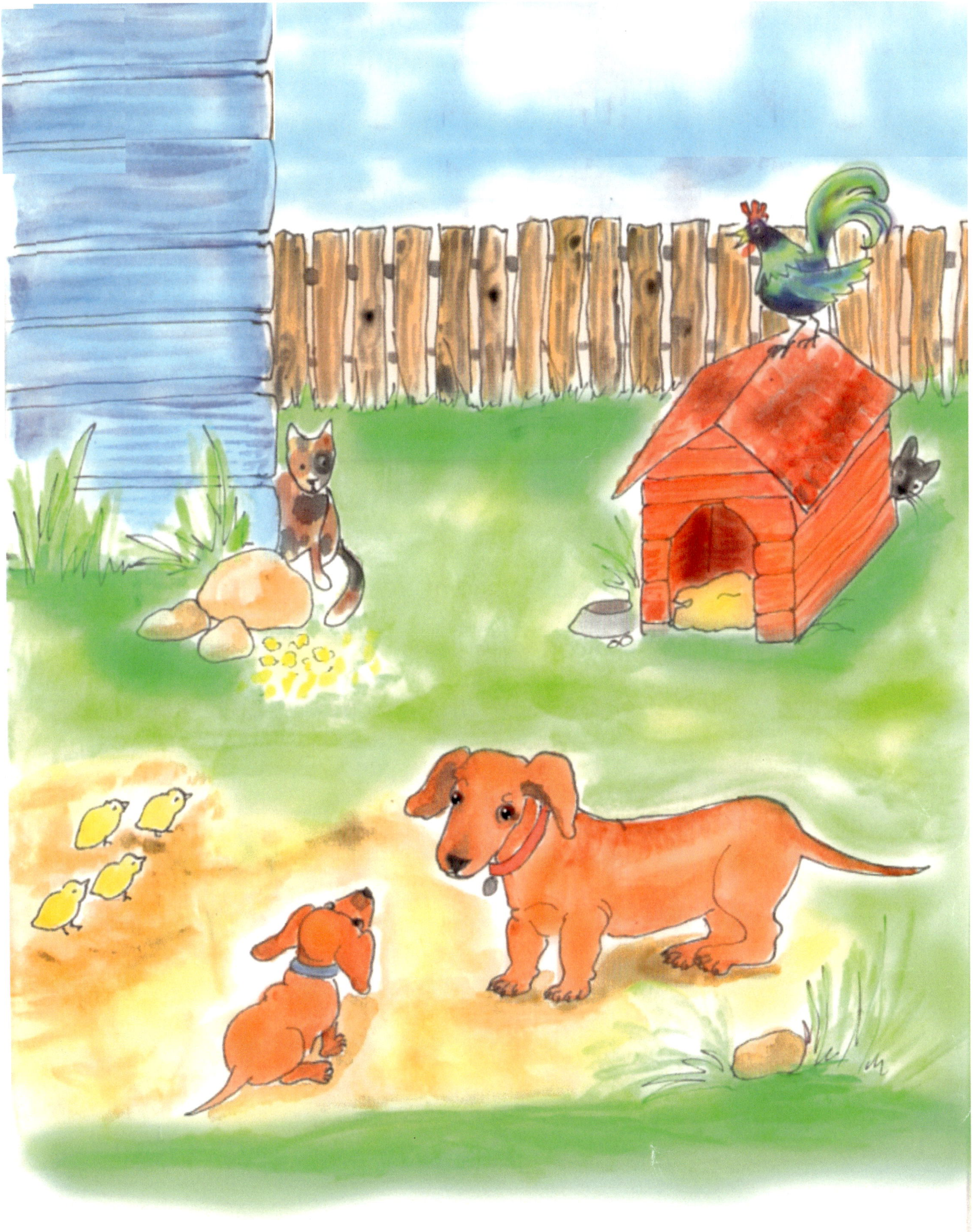

Harley went outside and immediately began looking for the feral cats. When he saw the big beautiful black one he remembered his promise to his mother and turned around and headed toward the other side of the yard. There he saw a tiny egg. Harley said to himself, "This egg is someone's baby."

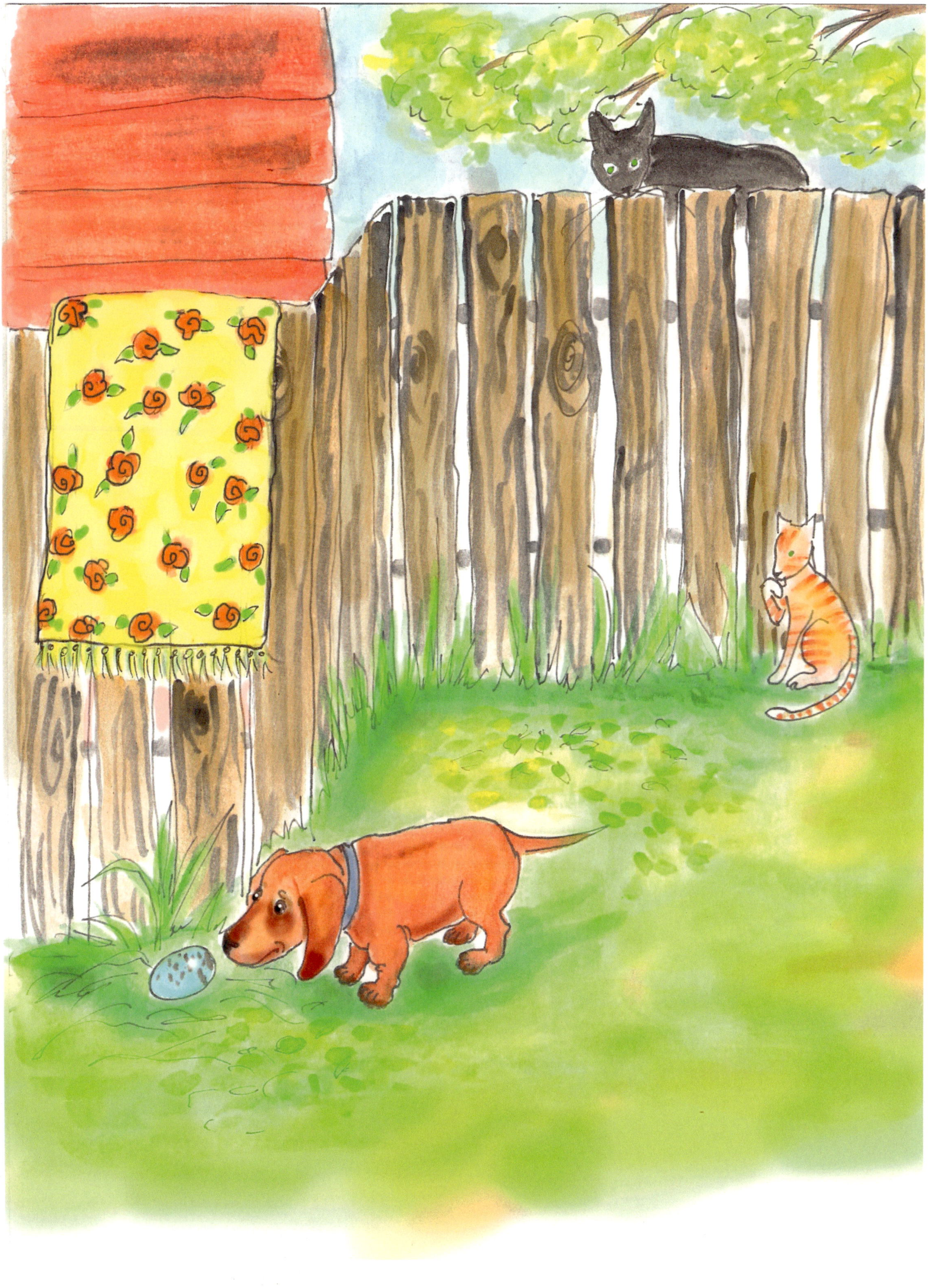

Harley carefully covered the egg with some leaves and grass that were lying near it and then excitedly ran to tell his mother about the egg.

"Mother, Mother!" exclaimed Harley as he ran inside the house. "Come see what I found!"

"Calm down Harley," responded his mother. "Now lead me to what you found."

Harley led his mother to the tiny egg that he had covered with leaves and grass. He said, "Mother, I found an egg. May I please keep it warm and hatch it like I've seen the chickens do? I want to be the daddy of whatever is in the egg since we don't know who its mother or daddy is. I'll be careful not to break it."

"Okay Harley. But first we will have to find a way to carefully move it to our house."

Harley saw a small, flat piece of wood and said, "Mother, maybe we can slide the egg onto this and then push it to the house. We can take turns pushing it with our noses. If we put enough leaves and grass under the egg then maybe it won't slide off."

"What a wonderful idea Harley. You're very smart."

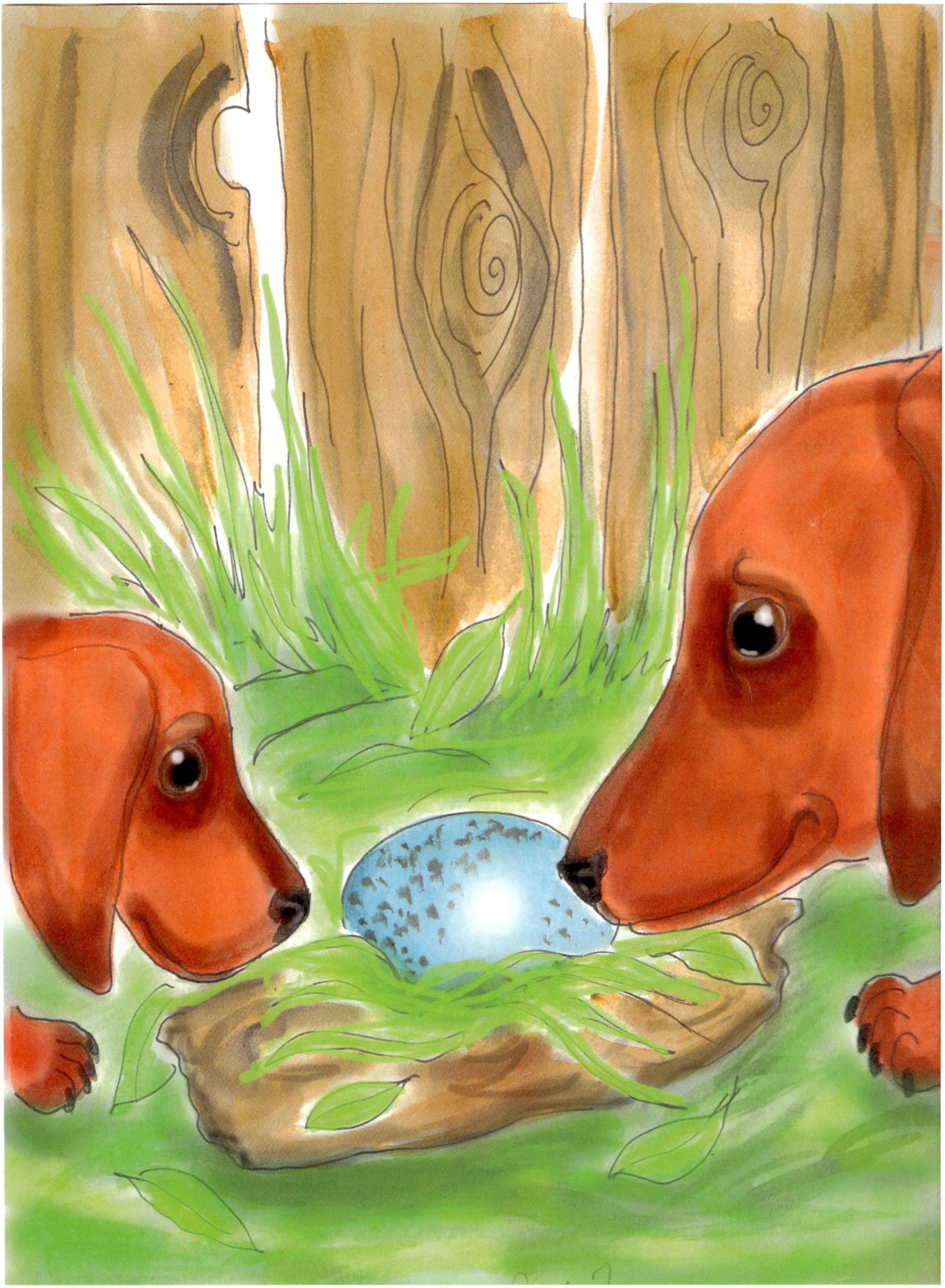

Harley and his mother successfully moved the tiny egg to their home and right away Harley began keeping the egg warm.

As soon as Harley and his mother moved the egg to their nice comfortable home, Harley lay down in a nice soft corner and his mother gently slid the egg off the flat piece of wood while being extra careful not to remove the leaves and grass that were covering it.

Harley lay very still as his mother put the egg as close to his warm little body as she could.

Harley kept the tiny egg warm for days, and only moved from his spot long enough to eat and use the bathroom, at which times his mother kept the egg warm with her body.

After days of Harley patiently waiting to be a daddy, the tiny egg finally hatched. Harley didn't know what had hatched from the egg but his mother said that it was a baby sparrow.

Harley said, "It's the most beautiful baby in the world and it's mine. I'll love my little baby sparrow forever."

"Harley, I guess you know that you will have to search for food for your little sparrow. It will have to be fed and watered because it's a living being."

"I know Mother. I'll take care of my baby just as you have always taken care of me. I'll be a good daddy."

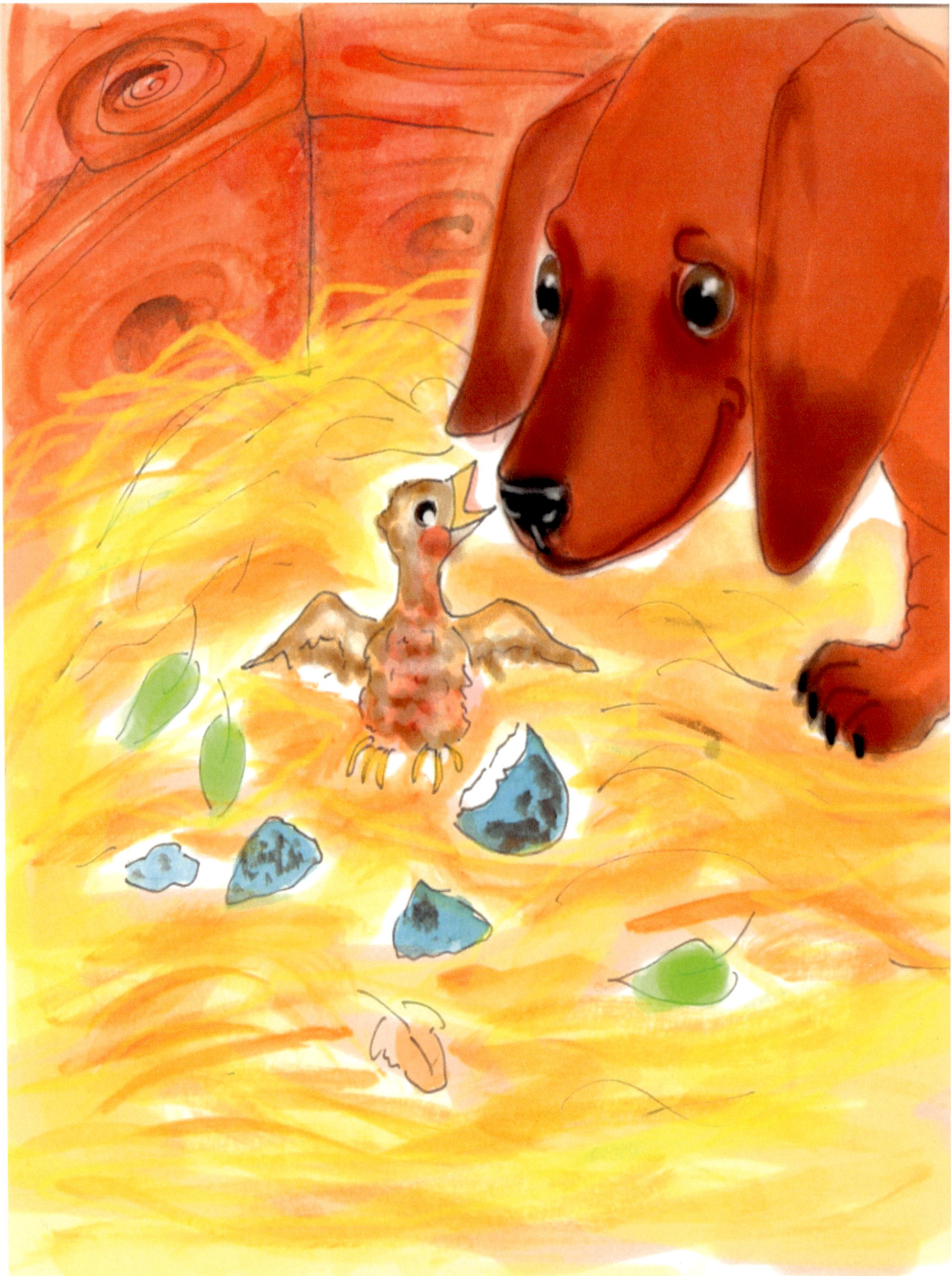

Harley searched for food for his little sparrow every day, and fed and watered it just like its mother would have done.

One day it occurred to Harley that he had not named his little bird. He told himself that he would talk to his mother about a name for his little bird.

The next day Harley said, "Mother, I need to name my baby. What should I name it?"

His mother said, "Think of a name that you think your baby would like when he grows up. I liked the name Harley and I thought you would too, so that's what I named you."

"I do like my name. I think I'll name my baby Sparky, because he just looks like a Sparky."

"I think that's a lovely name."

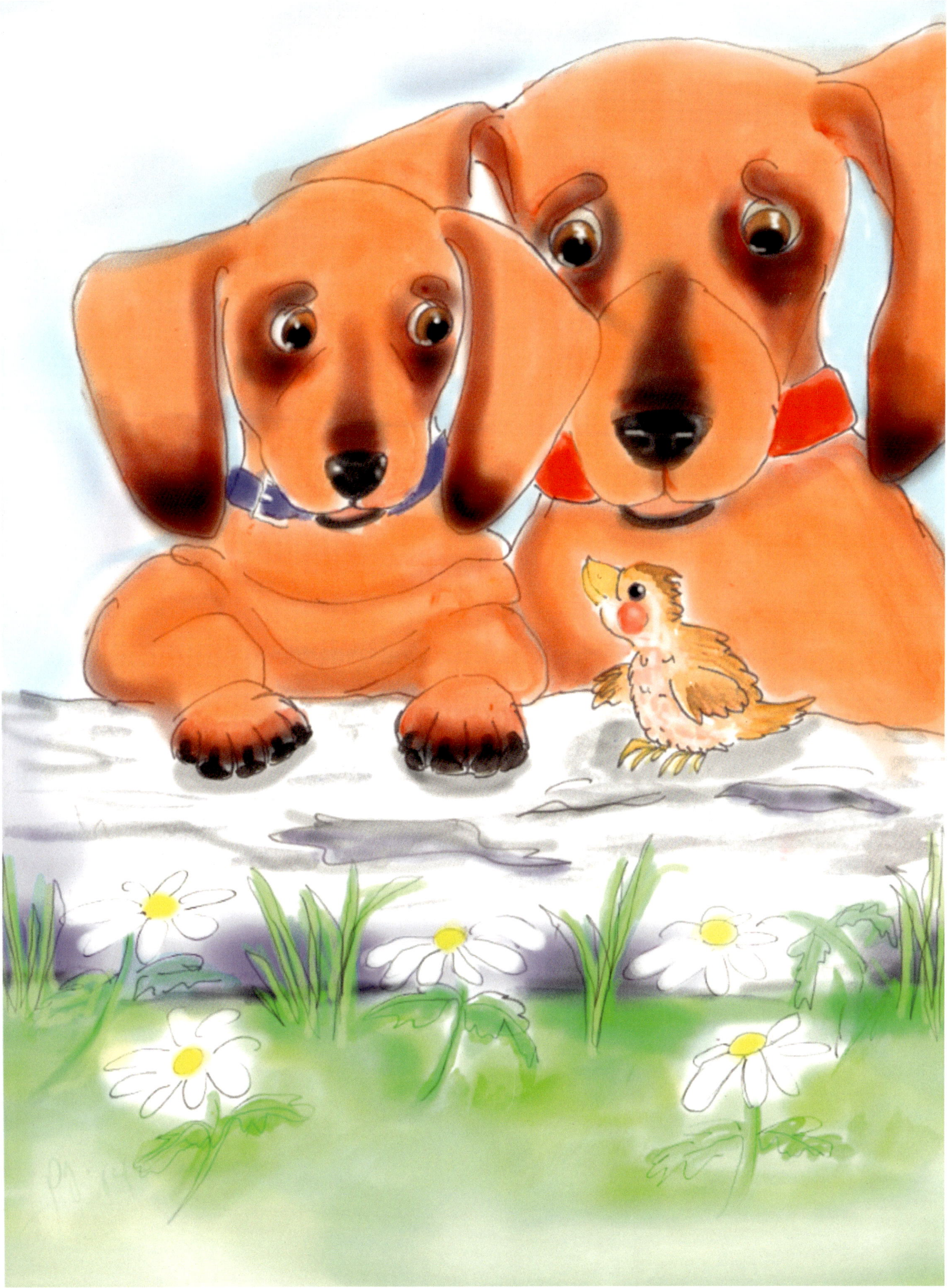

"There's something I need to tell you Harley."

"What's that, Mother?"

"I'll tell you after you feed Sparky."

"Okay Mother."

Harley's mother was concerned about how he would react to what she had to say. She had raised Harley to be thoughtful, loving, and caring, and he was all of those things, and she was very proud of him. She said to herself, "I'll just have to tell him what I must tell him and hope that he will understand."

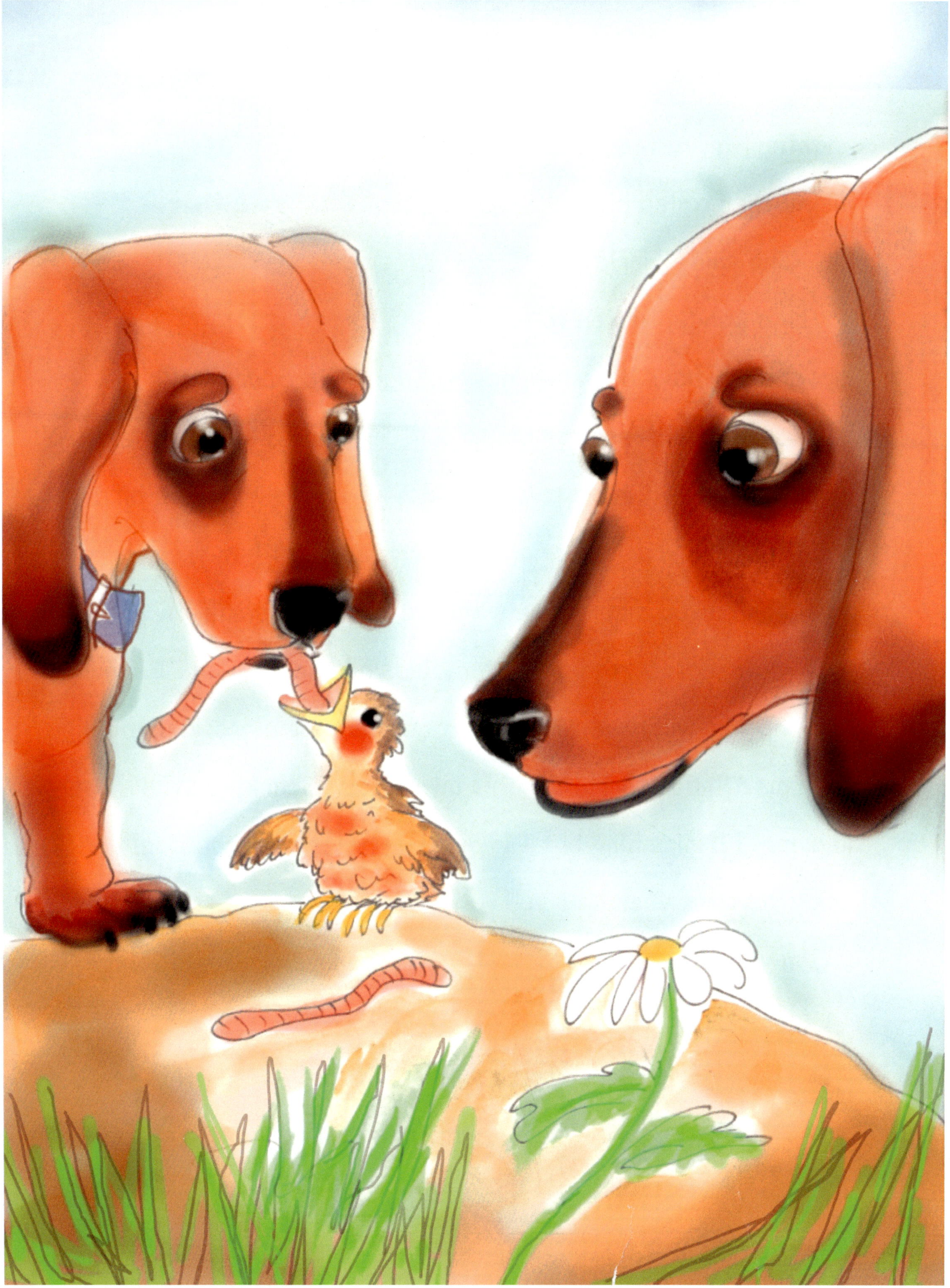

After Harley fed Sparky, his mother called him to her. She said, "Harley, you're a wonderful son to me, and you have been a wonderful daddy to Sparky. What I have to say isn't easy for me to say, but I must say it. One day very soon you will have to say goodbye to Sparky. He's a bird and birds fly. His mother and father would set him free if they had raised him, so you will have to do the same thing."

"I know that, Mother. I watch birds all the time and I know that Sparky will have to leave his nest and be a grown up bird and raise little sparrows of his own. I love Sparky just like you love me. I'll miss him, but I know that he won't forget me. He'll come visit me when he can."

"I'm very proud of you, Harley. You're more grown up than I thought you were."

It made Harley very happy to hear his mother say that she was proud of him. He said, "Thank you, Mother."

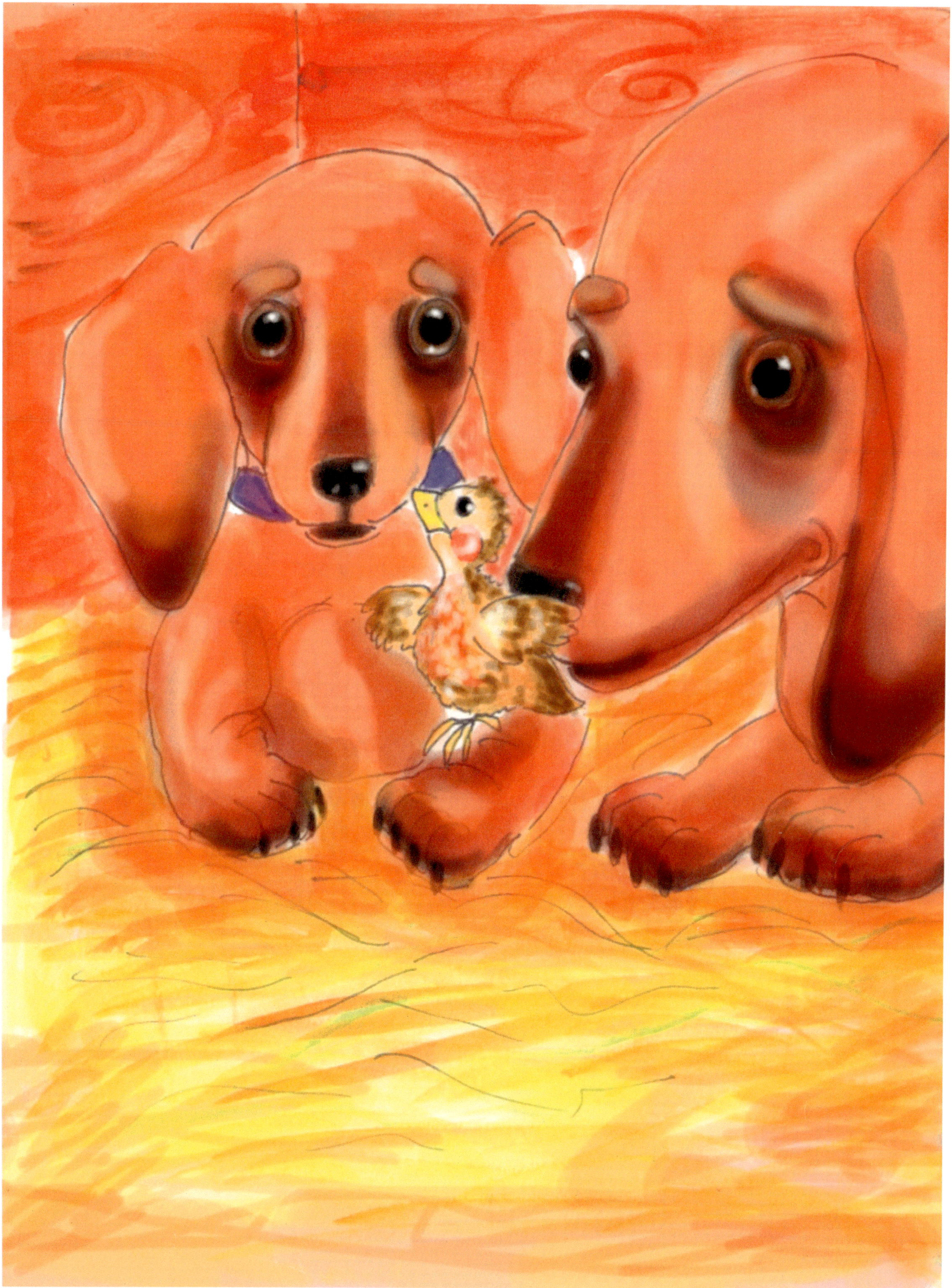

One beautiful sunny summer day Harley set Sparky free. Sparky flew upon Harley's back and flapped his little wings and flew away and then came back and sat on Harley's head. Harley knew that Sparky was telling him goodbye, so he said, "I love you, Sparky. You may go now. I'm setting you free. Please visit me when you can."

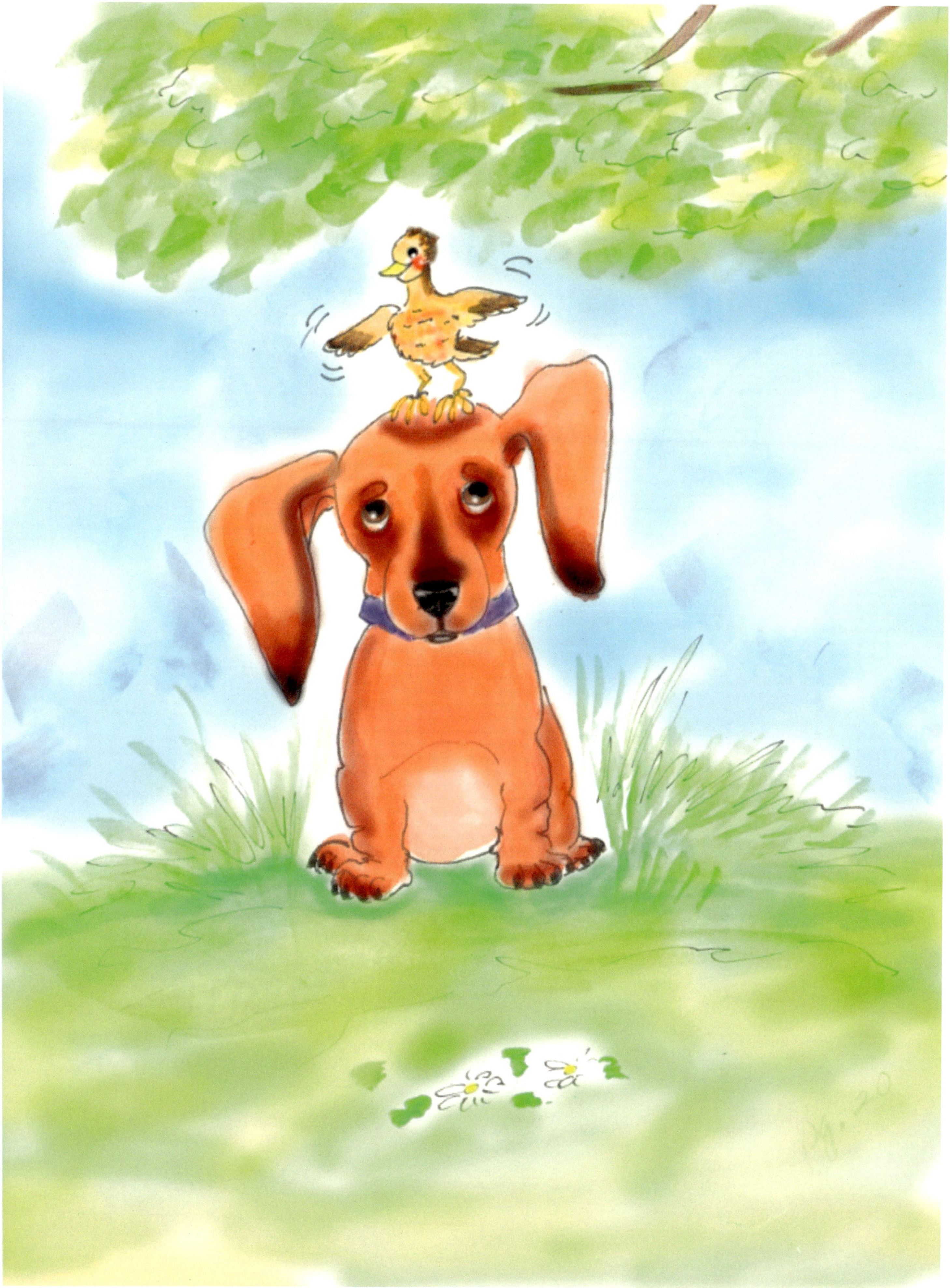

After Sparky flew away Harley's mother walked up to him and kissed him and said, "Harley, I am so proud of you. You behaved like a parent today. You loved Sparky enough to set him free."

"Now I know how much you love me."

"That's right Harley. Now you know how much I love you."

"That's a lot of love, too."

"It sure is, Harley."

Sparky still visits Harley, but now he brings his wife and babies. Seeing how much Sparky loves his family makes Harley very happy.

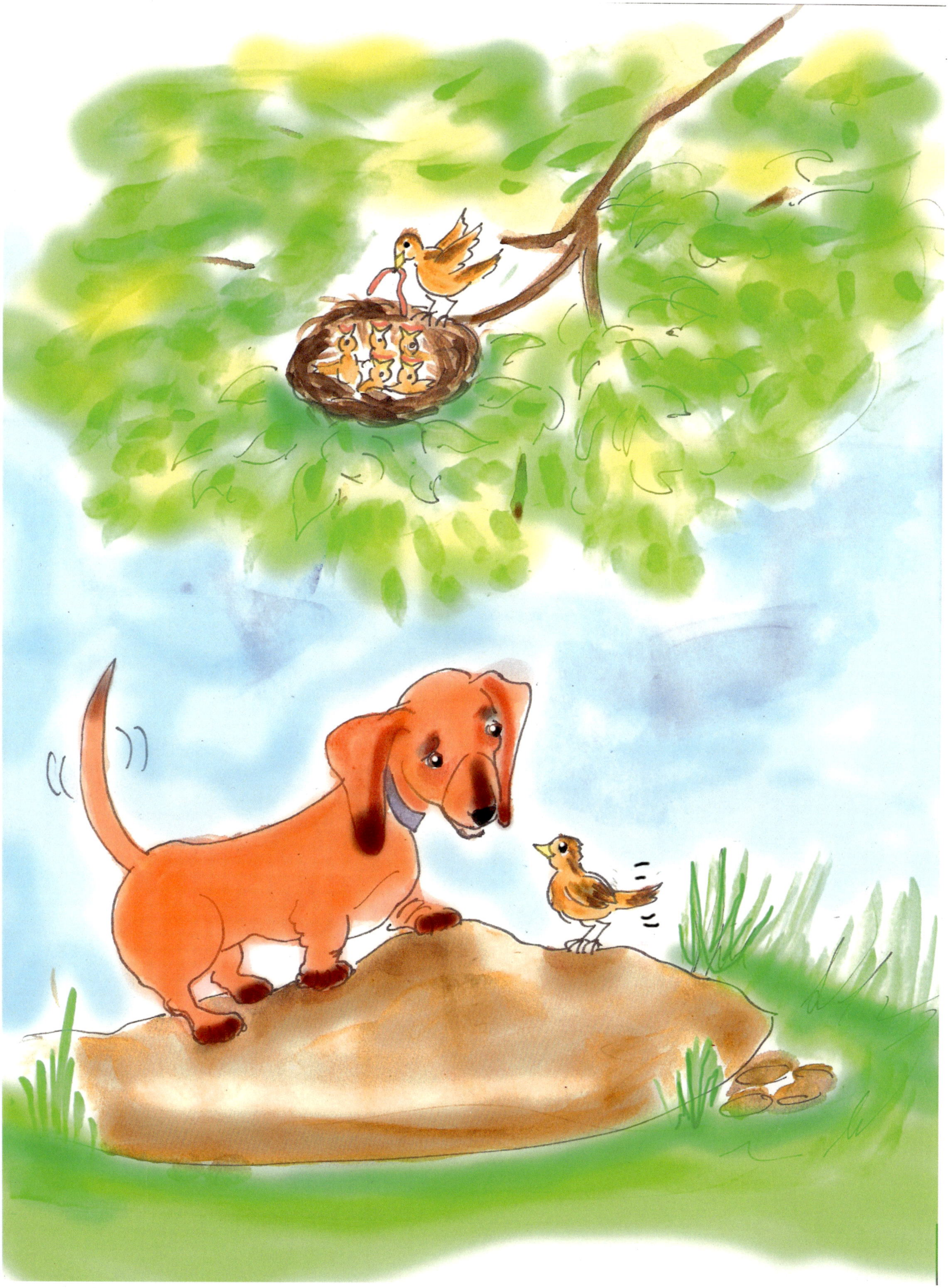

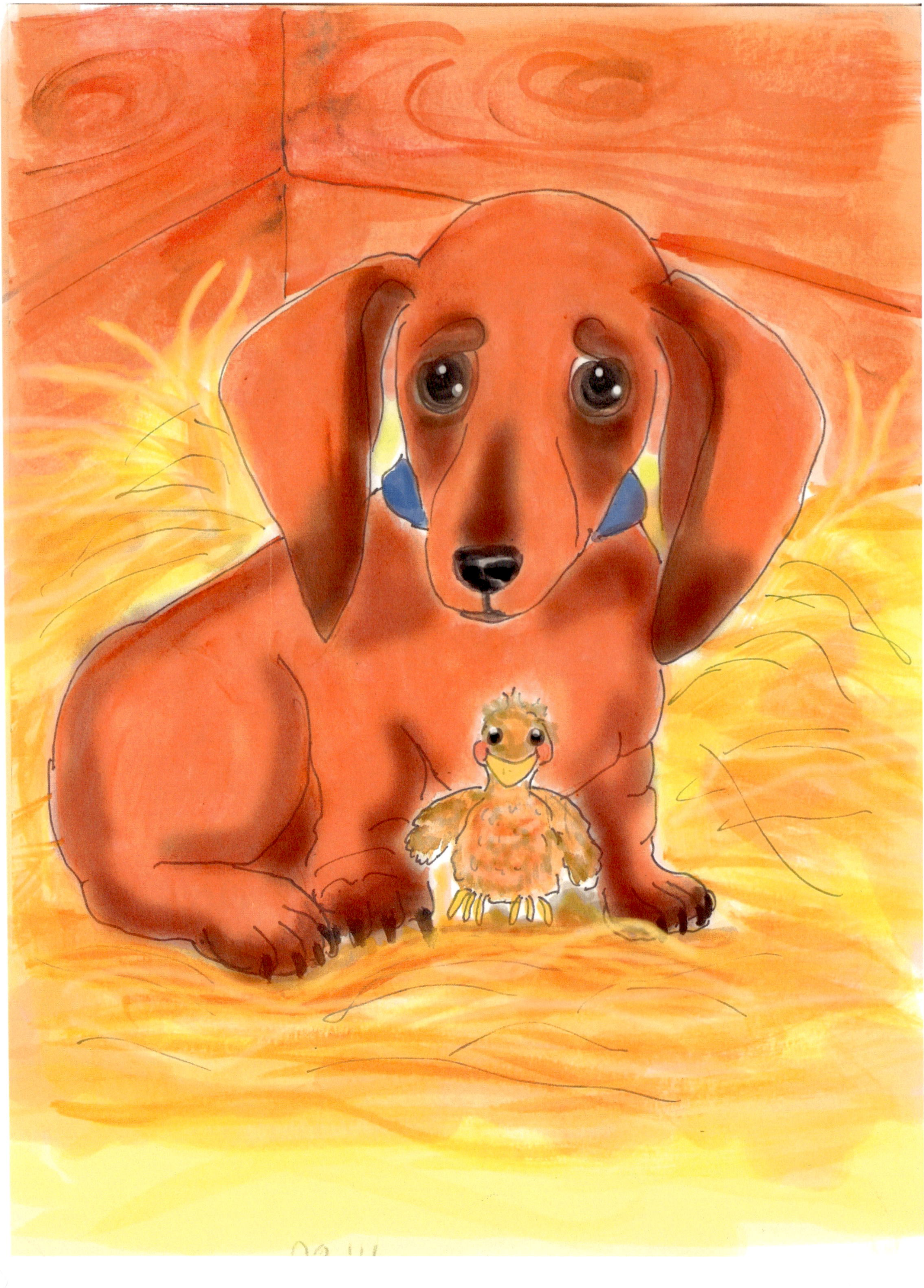

The End

Made in the USA
Columbia, SC
04 April 2019